nickelodeon

PAW PATROL™

Pups Fight Fire

PaRragon

Bath · New York · Cologne · Melbourne · Delhi
Hong Kong · Shenzhen · Singapore

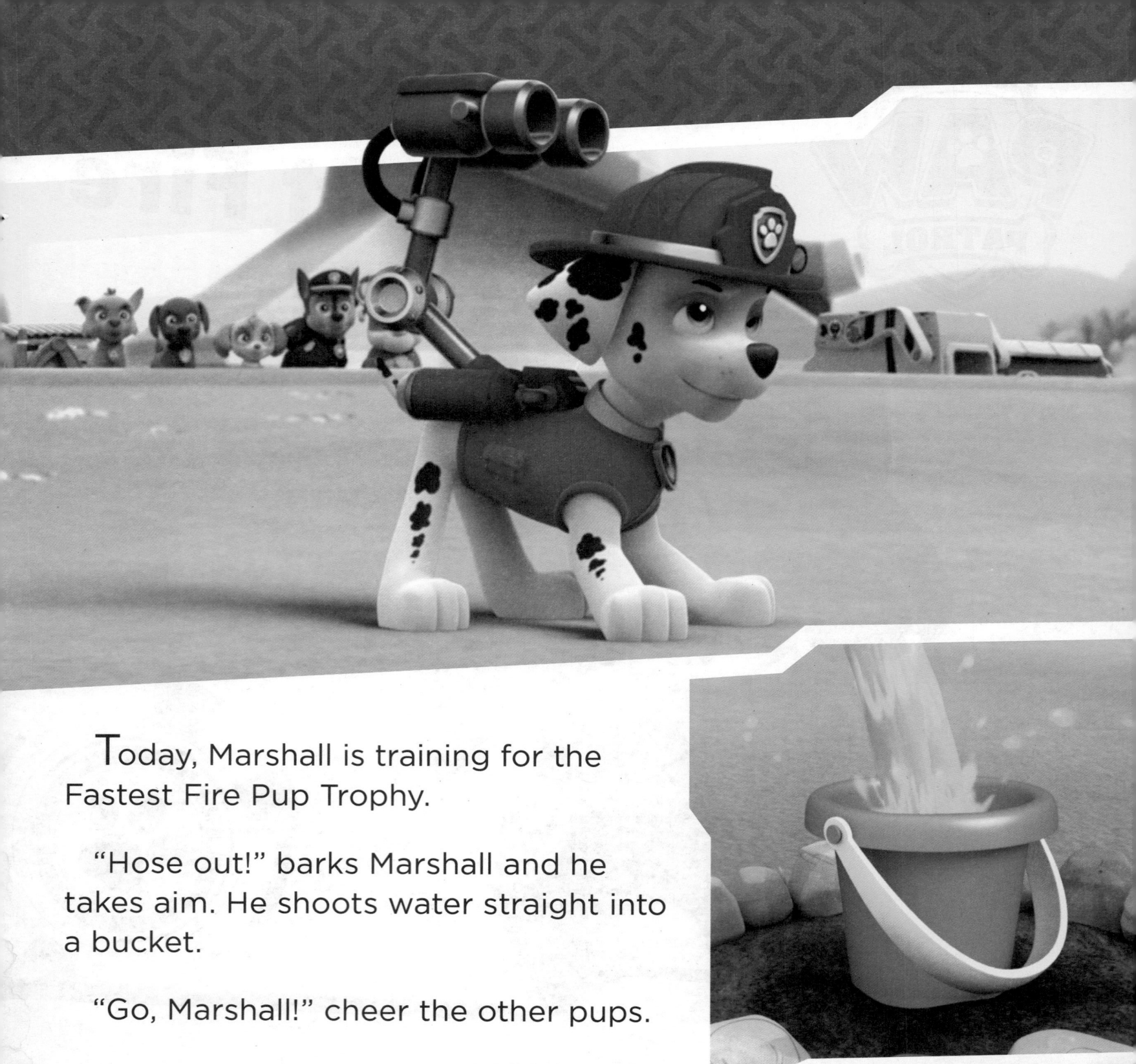

Today, Marshall is training for the Fastest Fire Pup Trophy.

"Hose out!" barks Marshall and he takes aim. He shoots water straight into a bucket.

"Go, Marshall!" cheer the other pups.

Next, Marshall drives his fire engine to a tree, to rescue Cali.

But the ladder hits the tree and Marshall falls with a BUMP!

Ryder is watching from the Lookout.

"It looks like Marshall could use a helping hand," he says, pushing a button on the PupPad.

"PAW Patrol to the Lookout!"

And with that, all the Pup Tags light up and the pups race to the tower.

In the control room, the pups line up, ready for action.

"Marshall, you need our help today," says Ryder. "But we just want you to try your best and not worry about winning."

"Try my best and forget the rest – OK!" says Marshall.

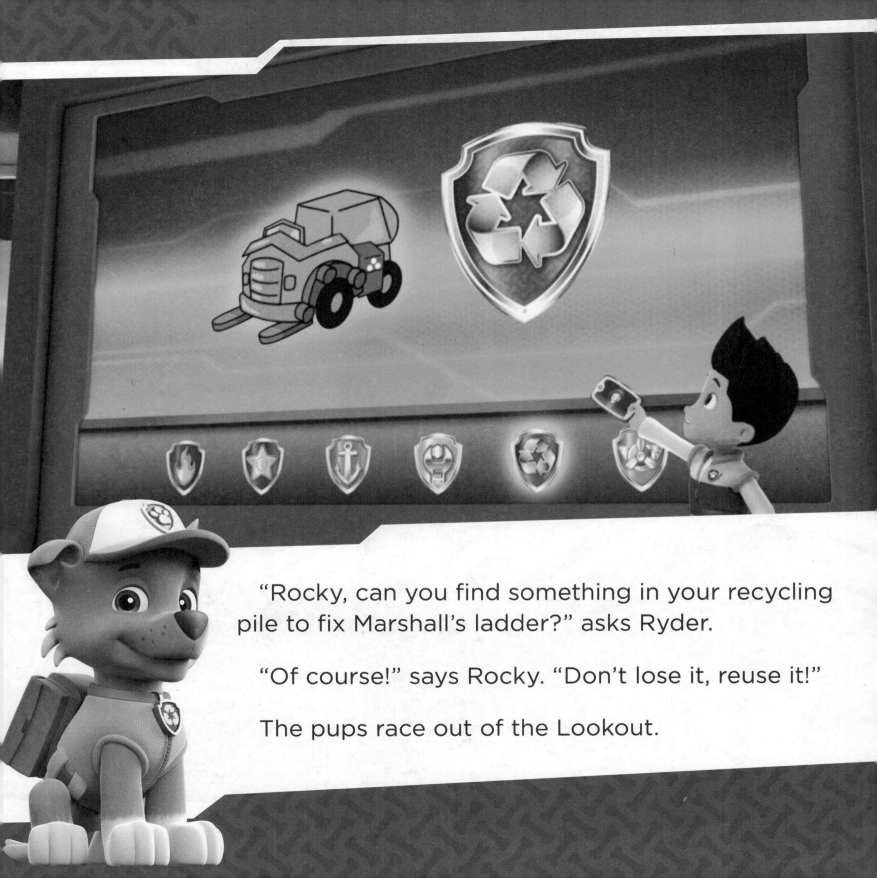

"Rocky, can you find something in your recycling pile to fix Marshall's ladder?" asks Ryder.

"Of course!" says Rocky. "Don't lose it, reuse it!"

The pups race out of the Lookout.

Rocky parks his truck next to Marshall's fire engine.
He finds something he can reuse.

"This broom will work," barks Rocky. "I'll use the handle to make new rungs for your fire ladder, Marshall."

Rocky screws the new rungs into place.

Ryder gets a call on the Pup Pad.

"There's a TV crew waiting to film Marshall break the Fastest Fire Pup record," says Mayor Goodway. "He's late!"

"Marshall's ready to go," says Ryder.

The PAW Patrol has to get Marshall
to the starting line right away.

Chase turns on the siren on his police truck and uses his traffic cones to clear the roads.

"My cones will stop the traffic until Marshall gets through," says Chase.

In the park, the TV crew are getting impatient. Marshall arrives just in time.

"You're on in three... two... one..." says the cameraman.

"Good morning, Adventure Bay!" says Mayor Goodway. "Today, Marshall the Fire Pup will attempt to win the trophy for completing the Fire Rescue Course in the fastest time ever!"

"Hooray! Go, Marshall!" the crowd cheers.

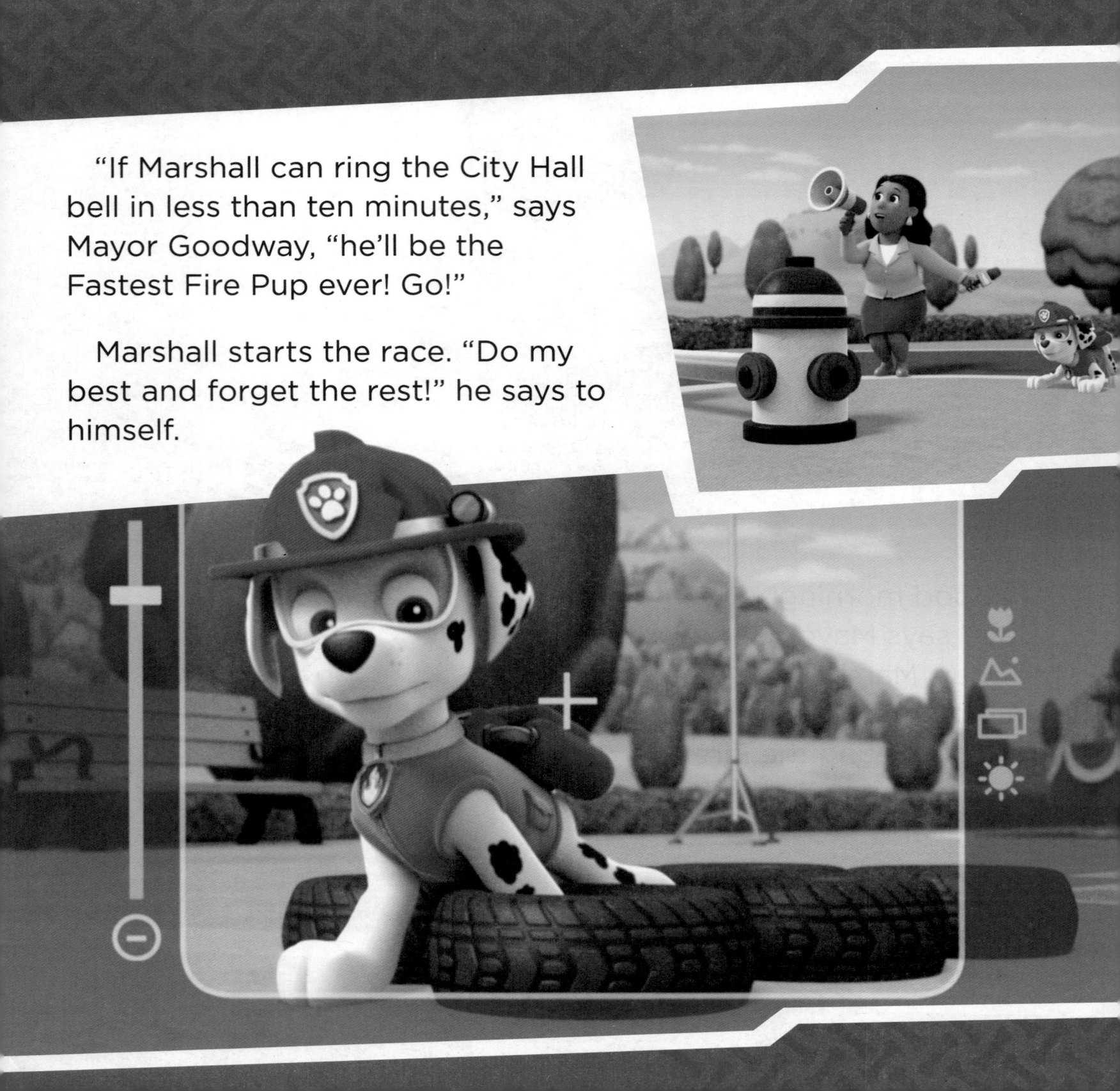

"If Marshall can ring the City Hall bell in less than ten minutes," says Mayor Goodway, "he'll be the Fastest Fire Pup ever! Go!"

Marshall starts the race. "Do my best and forget the rest!" he says to himself.

First he completes the obstacle course. Then, he uses his ladder. The new rungs mean that Marshall can easily reach the tree and rescue the toy cat.

Marshall races to the next task on the Beach Boardwalk.

"Hose out!" barks Marshall. He takes aim and the stream of water puts out a fake campfire.

Everyone cheers.

"I did it!" says Marshall. "Now I just have to get to City Hall and ring the bell."

But just as Marshall is about to get in his truck, he spots a real fire.

"Fire!" barks Marshall. "I'll take care of that. Hose on!"

Marshall puts out the fire with his Pup Pack hose.

"Thank you so much, Marshall," says Mayor Goodway.

"You've only got thirty seconds left now, Marshall!"
calls Ryder. "Go for it!

At City Hall, Marshall races up his ladder to the bell tower. He rings the bell.

DONG!

But he's one minute late! He hasn't broken the record.

"But Marshall, you stopped to put out a *real* fire," says Mayor Goodway, "and that makes you an Adventure Bay HERO!"

The Mayor presents him with the trophy. "For the *Greatest* Fire Pup in the World!" she says, and everyone cheers.

Later, back at the Lookout, the PAW Patrol is watching Marshall on the news.

"You did it, Marshall!" the pups shout.

Marshall is very proud of his trophy. "I really did my *best*!" he says.